And he was so small that I could
dress him up in my doll's clothes.

Hi! I'm Emily Elizabeth and
I want to show you some special
pictures of my dog Clifford.
You'll notice that he has grown up a lot!

When Clifford was a puppy,
he was so tiny that I had to
feed him with my doll's bottle.

He was just the right size for my electric toy car.

And he liked to hide in my dollhouse.

But I had to be careful when
I played with Clifford.

Even the smallest collar I could
find was too big for him.

And when he began to eat dog food,
I had to watch him all the time.

My puppy's first snow day
was a big adventure.

Here is a picture of a snowman I made with my friend.

I wanted Clifford to be in the picture, too.

Do you know what?

He was!

Clifford was always getting lost.

One time, he got lost at the post office.

Can you see my small red puppy?

Everyone cheered when we found him!

In this picture, Clifford was playing football.

Clifford even scored a touchdown!

Here I was making valentines.

Clifford made one, too!

When summer came, Clifford chased birds.
But he never caught one.

In autumn, Clifford chased falling leaves.
He had fun!

On Halloween, Clifford liked
the Jack-o'-lantern.

Clifford was the littlest ghost
I had ever seen.

That Halloween, Clifford discovered candy apples.

The candy was sort of sticky!

Before Christmas, Clifford helped
me wrap presents.

Clifford's first present from Santa was a bone.

For the new year, we had a wonderful surprise.

Clifford began to grow.

He grew some more.

And he grew some more.

We had to move from the city to the country.
This picture shows Clifford on moving day.

And this is Clifford all grown up.
I love my big red dog!

Look for the pictures from
Clifford Grows Up
in these other funny books.

Clifford's Puppy Days

Clifford The Small Red Puppy

Clifford's First Christmas

Clifford's First Snow Day

Clifford's First Valentine's Day

Clifford's First Autumn

Clifford's First Halloween

Clifford's Family

Happy Reading!

20 19 18 17 16 15 14 13 12   03 04 05 06 07 08

Printed in the U.S.A.
First printing, April 1999

NORMAN BRIDWELL

Clifford®
GROWS UP

SCHOLASTIC INC.
New York   Toronto   London   Auckland   Sydney